When Daddy's Truck Picks me up

Jana Novotny Hunter

Illustrated by Carol Thompson

www.av2books.com

Your AV² Media Enhanced book gives you a fiction readalong online. Log on to www.av2books.com and enter the unique book code from this page to use your readalong.

AV² Readalong Navigation

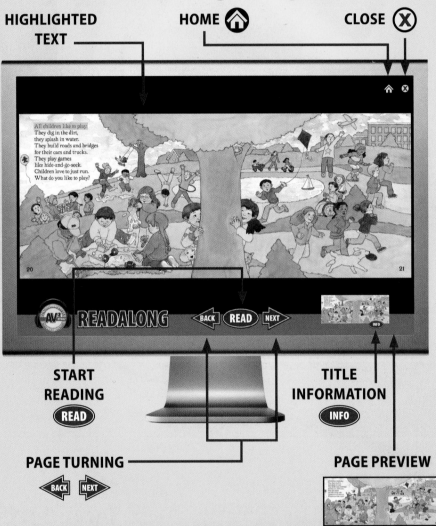

HIGHLIGHTED TEXT

HOME

CLOSE

START READING
READ

PAGE TURNING
BACK NEXT

TITLE INFORMATION
INFO

PAGE PREVIEW

Go to **www.av2books.com**, and enter this book's unique code.

BOOK CODE

K218835

AV² **by Weigl** brings you media enhanced books that support active learning.

First Published by

ALBERT WHITMAN & COMPANY
Publishing children's books since 1919

Published by AV² by Weigl
350 5th Avenue, 59th Floor New York, NY 10118
Websites: www.av2books.com   www.weigl.com

Library of Congress Control Number: 2014907242

ISBN 978-1-4896-2834-3 (hardcover)
ISBN 978-1-4896-2835-0 (single user eBook)
ISBN 978-1-4896-2836-7 (multi-user eBook)

Printed in the United States of America in North Mankato, Minnesota
1 2 3 4 5 6 7 8 9 0   18 17 16 15 14

Text copyright ©2006 by Jana Novotny Hunter.
Illustrations copyright ©2006 by Carol Thompson.
Published in 2006 by Albert Whitman & Company.

042014
WEP080414

For Flynn —J.N.H

For Leon and his dad —C.T.

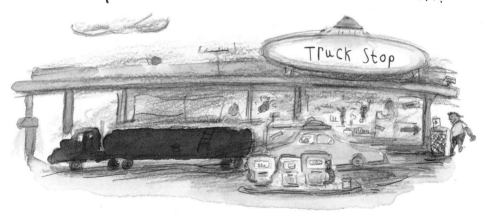

Truck Stop

Daddy and Me

me in my daddy's truck

Rig of the year

It's Daddy's turn to pick me up.
I get up fast today!
Daddy drives a tanker truck,
and he comes a long, long way.

I love to ride in Daddy's truck.
He picks me up from school.
Then I have Dad to myself.
We think that's *SOOO* COOl!

My daddy's picking me up today.
I'll wave Mom a big goodbye.
I just can't wait. Just can't wait!
Daddy's coming, that's why!

Heading down the highway
with his engine thumping—,
RRROar rrrumble RRROAR!
My daddy's coming!

When it's Daddy's turn to pick me up, I make the day go zoom!
I drive my big red tanker truck—
it's my time with Daddy soon.

Thundering through the tunnel, headlights help to see.

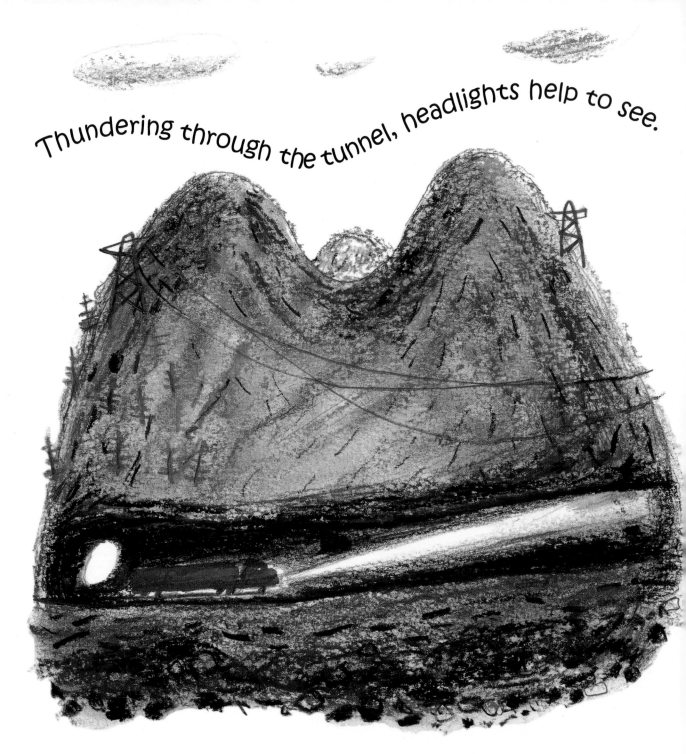

Bursting out the other end—Daddy's coming for me!

Crawling through my tunnel,
burrowing like a mole.
Going darker and deeper,
into the big, big hole.

Zooming zig-zag down the hill, singing our favorite tune. Rocking, rolling, roaring—Daddy'll be here soon!

I'm waiting and waiting *so* hard.
I hum our favorite song.
Humming through my sandwich,
"Daddy, don't be long!"

Filling up his fuel tank,
checking the tanker's load,
getting something just for me—
then Daddy's back on the road.

When Daddy picks me up,
I paint his smile, big as can be!
It's bursting off the paper,
the way Dad smiles at me!

Shifting down to first gear,
taking that bridge real s-l-o-w . . .
Crawling like a giant snail,
still a way to go.

School's getting out now.
The grownups are on time.
They wave and kiss and pick up their kids.
All the daddies—where's mine?

Honk, honk!

Beep, beep!

Stuck in heavy traffic,
engine running hot.
Grinding down. Braking hard.
Slowing to a stop!

Oh, no!

I'm making Daddy hurry up.
C'mon Dad, don't be slow.
I'm waiting hard. I want you *now.*
I really need us to go!

When is Daddy coming?   Soon.

23

When??

scrreeeech!

made it!

Then Daddy picks me up.
He swings me round and round.
And it's me and Dad—
Daddy and meeeeee—

WHEE·EEE·EEEEE!

Now we are together—
we won't wait one more minute.
Daddy's truck takes off so fast,
with me and Daddy in it!

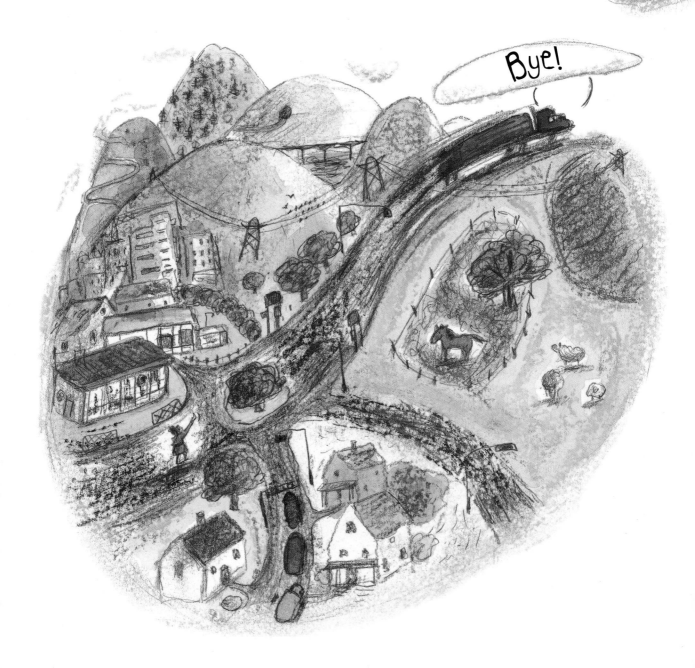